WHY DID THE HAGGIS CROSS THE ROAD?

and other Scottish jokes

Crombie Jardine Publishing Limited
4 Belgrave Place
Edinburgh EH4 3AN
Scotland
www.crombiejardine.com

First published by Crombie Jardine
Publishing Limited, 2008
Copyright © Crombie Jardine
Publishing Limited, 2008

ISBN 978-1-906051-26-6

Written by Stuart McLean
Proofread by Mandy Jardine
Design and typesetting by Mathew Lyons
Printed and bound in the UK by CPI William Clowes

Contents

Introduction

Scotland is an amazing, unique country with so much to celebrate. We have spectacular islands, mountains, glens and lochs. We have a wonderful culture of music, poetry and dance. We have a national football squad that can hold its own against some of the best Girl Guide teams in the world. We have a proud, though sometimes tragic, history. And if that's not enough, we have haggis, the Loch Ness Monster, kilts, whisky, Irn-Bru, heather, shortbread, tartan, thistles, bagpipes and so on and so on. But there's one thing we as a nation do particularly well – we love to take the piss out of all of this! Yes – when the people of Scotland tell a joke it's usually at our own expense. This book is a collection of Scottish jokes – some are old favourites retold, others are brand new and a few are crap specimens found on that internet thingy which have been massaged to make them funny. So whether you're Scottish, English, American, Canadian or come from Tuvalu, you're sure to laugh your socks off at this collection of Scottish jokes.

Apology

The author would like to apologise for the blatant and unprovoked use of the word 'dog' in this book.

Haggis Jokes

Haggis – the icon of the Scottish nation: oatmeal, plus the lungs, heart and liver of sheep with a large dash of blood, all stuffed into the poor creature's stomach! No wonder we're always so bloody miserable.

Tam walks into his local fish and chip shop.

"Two haggis suppers, Toni!" he calls across the counter.

"Och, you're really pushing the boat out tonight," says Toni. "Did you win the lottery?"

"Naw," says Tam, "but I did win third prize in a Sunny Govan Radio contest. Here's the voucher for my grub."

"Well done, mate," says Toni. "So what were the other prizes?"

"Second prize was a single haggis supper," says Tam.

"And first prize?" enquires Toni.

"Jist the chips," says Tam.

A haggis goes into a pub and orders a bottle of the best whisky.

"You're looking awfy smug wae yerself," says the barman.

"Aye," says the haggis, "Ah've jist been sewing ma wild oats."

Q. What do you call a haggis in the Sahara desert?
A. Lost.

A haggis makes his way down through the heathery hillside of Loch Ness and, after a wee drink from the loch, he sits on a stone with his feet chilling in the water. Within minutes a busload of American tourists has gathered round snapping photos of the cute little creature. After a while one of the tourists asks, "Have you ever spotted the monster?"

"Och, no," says the haggis, "and to be honest, I don't really believe in him."

Three haggis are having a night on the town. At chucking out time they buy a carry-out and head home to continue the party. On the way, the first haggis suggests getting some kebabs.

"No' for me," said the second.

"Oh, come on," said the third, "jist have a wee yin."

"Ah cannae," said the second, "I'm a veggie haggis."

Bessie haggis is sitting at the disco
minding her own business when this
black pudding comes up to her and asks,
"Ur ye dancin'?"

Bessie looks him up and down, "Naw
Ah'm no' ya big bloody puddin'," she
retorts.

Nessie Jokes

Nessie is lying at the bottom of the loch moaning to his wife.

"Ma bloody stomach is aching," he grumbles.

"Och it serves you right, for eating them American tourists," replies Mrs Ness. "You know they're far too rich for you."

Q. What's big and white and chills out at the bottom of Loch Ness?
A. The Loch Ness Refrigerator.

A lady goes into a bar with Nessie on a leash. The bartender looks over and says, "Hey, you cannae bring that ugly fat pig in here."

"Excuse me," said the lady indignantly, "but if you'd put your glasses on you'd see that this is the Loch Ness Monster."

"Ah wisnae talkin' tae you," says the barman, "Ah wis talkin' tae the monster."

Q. How do you know if the Loch Ness Monster is under the bed?
A. Your face is squashed against the ceiling.

Q. What's fifty metres long, scary, and sings *Scotland the Brave*?
A. The Loch Ness Songster.

A haggis and the Loch Ness Monster are playing golf when a group of Canadians spots them.

"Isn't the little fella awful cute in his kilt?" says the first.

"Gee, we must get our photos taken with them," says the second.

Soon the whole group is gathered round taking snap after snap after snap. Finally they all hurry off to catch their bus. As they leave one calls to Nessie, "Hey bud, what's your handicap?"

"Stupid bloody tourists!" replies Nessie.

Q. How can you tell if Nessie is in your fridge?
A. There's no bloody food left.

Q. What's huge, yellow, lives at the bottom of Loch Ness and has never been seen?
A. The Loch Ness Canary.

Peter, a lifelong atheist, is fishing when Nessie attacks his boat. In one playful flip, the beast tosses him and his boat a hundred feet into the air.

As Peter tumbles towards the monster's open jaws he cries out, "Oh, my God! Help me!"

Suddenly, the scene freezes and, as Peter hangs in mid-air, a voice booms from above, "Ah thought ye didnae believe in me!"

"God, gies a break!" says Peter. "Minutes ago Ah didnae even believe in the Loch Ness Monster."

"Well," says God, "Ah'm so glad ye've been converted at last."

"Gonnae no' let thon monster eat me," says Peter.

"Ah can only dae miracles on Sunday," says God. "Sorry an' that."

"Come oan," pleads Peter, "Ye must be able tae dae something."

"Aye okay then," says God, "Ah'll make Nessie believe in me – maybe then he'll take pity on you."

"Aw thanks a bunch," says Peter.

The scene starts in motion again with Peter falling towards Nessie. As he plunges into its huge mouth he hears it say, "Lord, bless this food Ye hae sae graciously provided…"

Q. Why did Nessie eat a halogen lamp?
A. Because he needed a light snack.

Kilts & Tartan Jokes

A Japanese businessman goes into a kilt maker's to enquire about having kilts made for his entire family. Realising that there's a massive profit to be made, the kilt maker is keen to get the sale.

"The only problem," says the businessman, "is that I don't expect we belong to any Scottish Clan."

"Actually you do," says the kilt-maker without hesitation, "Tokushimanachahati is part of the MacGullible Clan – we have plenty of tartan in stock."

For his eighteenth birthday a rich aunt gives Paul a bale of tartan and money to have a kilt made. He goes to a kilt maker and gets measured up. As he's a bit shy he asks the kilt maker to make some matching undies. Two weeks later Paul goes back to the shop.

"Your kilt and underwear are ready," says the kilt maker, "and there was five yards of material left over."

"That's grand," replies Paul. "Maybe I could get my girlfriend a matching kilt."

Paul rushed home. Excitedly he pulls on the kilt. He loves it so much he immediately dashes round to show his girlfriend. Unfortunately, in his excitement, he forgets to don his underwear.

When his girlfriend answers the door, Paul does a twirl and says, "Well, what do you think?"

"Wow!" she exclaims.

"But here's the biggest surprise…" he cries, yanking up the kilt. "Have you ever seen anything like that?"

"Oh, my God," says his girlfriend, "that's amazing."

"Well I've got five more yards at home," says Paul eagerly, "I'd be happy to let you have it anytime!"

A man walks into a pub with an octopus. He sits the octopus down on a stool and tells everyone in the pub that this talented animal can play any musical instrument in the world.

Everyone in the pub laughs, calling him an idiot. So he says that he will pay £20 to anyone with an instrument that the octopus can't play.

A Welshman walks up with a guitar and sets it beside the octopus. Immediately the octopus picks up the guitar and starts playing better than Segovia. The Welshman hands over his £20. An Englishman walks up with a trumpet. This time the octopus plays the trumpet better than Miles Davis. So the Englishman also hands over his £20.

Then a Scotsman walks up with some bagpipes. He gives them to the octopus and the octopus fumbles around with them in a confused fashion for several minutes.

"Ha!" says the Scot. "Can ye nae play it?"

The octopus looks up at him and says, "Play it? I'm going to make love to it as soon as I figure out how to get its pyjamas off!"

Jock was in London wearing his tartan when a curious lady asked if there was anything worn under the kilt.
'No madam,' he replied with a flourish.
'Everything is in perfect working order.'

KILT, n. A costume sometimes worn by Scotchmen in America and Americans in Scotland.

Ambrose Bierce

James, a young Scotsman was at a party in Edinburgh, dressed in his kilt, as were most of the men there. He fancied a girl at the party but didn't have the nerve to ask her to dance. Just as the last song came on, she approached him and asked, "Would you like to dance with me?"

Very pleased she'd made the first move, James responded, "Aye, how could you tell?"

"By the gleam in your eye," she said.

After they had danced the last dance she asked him, "Would you like to walk me home?"

James eagerly responded, "Aye, how could you tell?"

"By the gleam in your eye," she said.

When they reached her house she calmly asked him, "Would you like to come in and sleep with me?"

James couldn't believe his luck but was curious this time, "Was it the gleam in my eye?"

"No," she responded, "just the wee tilt in your kilt."

Some Lesser-Known Tartans

All Breeds Dairy Goats Tartan
Originally designed for a sash to be awarded to the Best Exhibit All Breeds Dairy Goats in the Gunnedah Show – now a must with all fashion-conscious bovines.

The Black Watch Shagging Tartan
The off-duty tartan of the Black Watch.

The Association of Wankers Tartan
Originally for the Association of Bankers but a typographical error made in 1913 gave the tartan a much more appropriate name.

Braveheart – Warrior Tartan
Believe it or not there really is a
Braveheart tartan! Mel Gibson has got a
lot to answer for.

Australian Donkey Tartan
Created for the Australian Donkey
Breeders to celebrate this wonderful
beast. The perfect tartan for making that
"I'm well hung" statement at a wedding.

Buckie Commando Tartan
A tartan only seen at Ned weddings –
perfect for Shuggie, Senga and their
three Nedette bridesmaids on that
special day. The full dress includes
tartan cap to be worn at a jaunty angle
and tartan trackies.

Salem Scottish Dancer's Wee Blue Tartan

Created for a Highland dance group in the Boston area, Massachusetts, USA in 1974. Hasn't the name got a beautiful ring to it?

Sikh Tartan

Designed to celebrate the 50th Anniversary of the arrival of A. J. Singh's family to Scotland. It includes blue for the Scottish flag, green for the Indian flag and the saffron of the Sikh community.

Virgin Tartan

With a tartan called Virgin you'd expect it to be white but no… it's bright red. You'd be far too embarrassed to wear it!

A group of Highland women is hurrying home to their wee but-and-bens after an afternoon bingo session. On the way down from one of the mountains (in the Highlands it's not uncommon to walk fifty miles over mountains to go to the bingo), they spot a man trapped under an avalanche of fallen rocks. As only his lower half is sticking out from the rocks they decide to lift his kilt and try to identify him.

"It's not my man," says Maggie, taking a wee peek.

"It's too big tae be ma Bertie," says Heather.

Morag pushes her friends aside and

takes a good, long hard look.

"Naah, it's okay girls," she declares, "he's not even from our village."

Young Rod got his first job, as a waiter working for an outside catering company. After a few days of training he's considered ready to be let loose on the public. The first function is a big, posh wedding in Milngavie and all the waiters have to wear kilts. But it's a stormy day and Rod is terrified for he's never worn a kilt before. As a precaution he stuffs his penis into a tea-cosy. Carrying his tray he heads out to serve the guests. As he approaches the bride's mother a gust of wind blows but Rod feels confident that nothing will show.

"Would you like some Champagne?" he asks politely.

"Not for me son," says the bride's mother, "but you can give me a cup of tea any day."

Assorted Jokes

Dundonian for Beginners
(Yer one stop guide tae ahin that's worth kenin aboot the lingo in Dundee.)

Floors	Smelly things that you give yer girlfriend on her birthday.
Hermless	Someone who has lost their Herms.
Hunners	Any quantity more than ten.
Jehkit	What yer mate holds for ye during a fight.

Naikit Something a Dundonian feels when he's not wearing his semmit.

Peece Staple diet of the masses – can be filled with jam, chips or even mince.

Windee A clear thing that lets you see out of yer hoos.

Q. Did you hear about the last wish of the hen-pecked husband of a house-proud Edinburgh wife?
A. He asked to have his ashes scattered on the carpet.

"They've goat a brilliant game at ma local pub," says Jock.

"Oh aye, whit's that?" asks Tam.

"Ye put on a blindfold an' drink a bottle o' whisky," says Jock, "then ye've goat tae try an' guess who ye are."

"Oh aye," says Tam.

"An' ye know," says Jock, "Ah've never guessed right once."

"Jimmy, dae you know yer wearing wan green sock and wan blue sock?" asks Malkie.

"Aye," replies Jimmy, "and dae you know Ah've got another pair exactly the same at hame."

Five a Day

The Scottish Government has come up with an alternative five-a-day foods list for healthy living that better reflects the Scottish lifestyle. These include the following:

❏ A bowl of porridge (the oats will keep you regular)

❏ At least four pints of beer (for the hops and malt)

❏ One deep fried Mars Bar (a Mars a day helps you work, rest and play)

❏ Six cans of Irn-Bru (great source of ammonium ferric citrate)

❏ A large portion of haggis, neeps and tatties (as neeps taste like shit you can skip these)

❏ Ten strawberry tarts (you need to get some fruit down you)

❏ Forty fags (tobacco is a herb after all!)

Hamish arrives in Glasgow after a long journey from Orkney. He's desperate for a drink so rushes into the first pub he sees. While ordering his drink he spots a rare bottle of 1968 Balvenie locked up behind the bar.

"And how much for a nip of that?" asks Hamish.

"Och that's no' fur sale," replies the barman, "but you can win it if you're really brave."

"Oh aye – and whit dae I have tae do?" asks Hamish.

"First you need tae gie Big Malkie a doin'," says the barman pointing at the six-foot, tattooed hard man propping up the other end of the bar.

"Oh aye," says Hamish all non-committal, downing his whisky.

"If you survive that," says the barman, "ye have tae pull out a rotting tooth frae ma pet dug." He opens the back door and there is the biggest, most savage, pit-bull that has ever graced the dog-fighting arenas of Glasgow.

"Oh aye," says Hamish all non-committal, downing another whisky.

"And then comes the worst part," says the barman, "ye need tae shag the arse aff ma mither-in-law."

"Whit's sae bad about that?" asks Hamish.

"Christ, she's got an uglier mug than Medusa," says the barman. "Wan look at her an' ye turn tae pure shite."

"Oh aye," says Hamish all non-committal, downing another whisky.

"So ur ye man enough for the task?" asks the barman.

"Aye nae bother," says Hamish, "but you'll have tae remind me of the tasks, ma memory's pure crap when Ah've hud a few."

The barman explains the tasks again and Hamish heads across to Big Malkie. Hamish yanks up his kilt to reveal the biggest todger in the whole of Scotland.

"What dae ye think of that then wee man?" says Hamish.

While Big Malkie stares in stunned amazement, Hamish whacks him over the head with his outsized tool. As the ambulance winds its way towards the wee pub, Hamish heads out to confront the dog. Everyone in the pub listens expectantly to the growls, groans, moans and snarling coming from the other side of the little door. After twenty minutes the door bursts open and Hamish staggers in, blood dripping from his arms and legs.

"Job done," he says, "now gies a pair of pliers."

"Whit?" exclaims the barman.

"Ah'll need some pliers fur the next task," says Hamish.

"Whit fur?" asks the barman.

"Tae fix thon bad tooth o' yer mither-in-law's," says Hamish.

Big Eck is flying off to New York to do his Christmas shopping. Strapping himself into his seat he's surprised to see a parrot hop onto the seat beside him. Politely Big Eck asks the stewardess for a coffee whereupon the parrot squawks in a broad Glaswegian accent, "An' get me a whisky ya bitch."

The flustered stewardess hurries back with a whisky but forgets Eck's coffee.

Apologetically Big Eck reminds the stewardess but, as she goes to get it, the parrot squawks, "Gies some Bucky toot-sweet honey."

Rather upset, the girl comes back shaking with the Buckie but still no coffee.

Annoyed at being ignored Big Eck tries the parrot's approach. "I've asked you politely for a coffee twice. So get it now ya bitch or Ah'll gie you a Glesga Kiss."

Moments later, two burly stewards throw Big Eck and the parrot out of the emergency exit. Plunging towards the ground the parrot turns to him and says, "See you, big man, fur someone who disnae fly, you're a ballsy bastard!"

The following was apparently seen on a poster outside a Scottish church in Arbroath: DRINK IS YOUR ENEMY.

Adjacent to this was another poster which said: LOVE YOUR ENEMY.

The 10 Silliest Scottish Names

Jock Strap

Skye Walker

Iona Weeboat

Tony MacAroni

Carol Singer

Farquar Hoffe

Shauna Legge

Duncan Macthegrassgrow

Isa Gower

Mac Macmac

"Hi mucker, Ah huvnae seen you fur yonks," says Ned 1.

"Aye – Ah've been away fur a while," says Ned 2.

"Oh ya beazer – did ye huv a good time?"

"Aye pure mental – apart frae huvvin' tae slop oot."

"Whit?" asks Ned 1 in astonishment. "Where wis ye – Barlinnie Prison?"

"Naw," says Ned 2, "Ah jist spent ra Glesga Fair doon it Butlins."

In an effort to reduce the number of fatal road accidents the Scottish Parliament recently had thousands of 'black boxes' installed into cars so they can find out why crashes happen. Strangely the last words of the driver varied remarkably from area to area. Here are some of the most common last words:

Bonnybridge: *What's that strange light in the sky? Is it a U. F. . . . Oooohhhh.*

Fort William: *Sure, Ah'm fine drivin' hefter two bottles o' whisky.*

John O'Groats: *Well according to the Sat-Nav the road goes north for another mile.*

Iona: *And with only five cars on the island you never meet any . . . waaahhhh.*

Glasgow: *Here, haud ma Buckie man and WATCH THIS!*

Strangest Scottish Place Names

Assloss (Ayrshire)

Backside (Banffshire)

Brawl (Highlands)

Buttock Point (Argyll & Bute)

Clappers (Borders)

Climpy (South Lanarkshire)

Cock Bridge (Aberdeenshire)

Cros (Isle of Lewis)

Hole of Bugars (Shetland Isles)

Kilmahog (Perthshire)

Lord Berkeley's Knob (Sutherland)

Lost (Aberdeenshire)

Ringburn (Dumfries and Galloway)

Rotten Bottom (Scottish Borders)

Spunkie (East Ayrshire)

Twatt (Orkney Islands)

Windy Yet (East Ayrshire)

Football Jokes

Q. Why have Stirling never won the
Scottish Cup?
A. Because every time they get a corner,
they put a fish and chip shop on it.

Having avoided employing any Catholic
players during their 100 year existence,
Tweedsville Rangers were keen to take
one on to prove that they weren't a
bunch of bastarding bigots. After
numerous committee meetings they
finally agreed to solve all their problems
in one go. They placed this advert in the

Glasgow Herald: "Catholic player wanted. Must be of mixed Black African and Jewish parentage. She should be registered blind and disabled with transvestite or lesbian orientation. Preference will be given to dyslexic applicants under 4ft who have a phobia of football."

Not all managers are as bright as one might hope. Apparently the boss of one Premier Division team, on seeing the headlines, 'Van Gogh up for sale at £10,000,000' rushed across to Paris in an attempt to sign him up.

I much prefer fantasy football to the real thing. My winning team is Angelina Jolie, Kelly Brook, Jessica Alba, Keira Knightley…

You know you're supporting Scotland's worst team if
… they play in 0-0-10 formation
… the digital scoreboard has three digits for opponents' goals
… you consider a 5-1 defeat a moral victory

… the referee apologises for every decision against your team
… the team pray before kick-off
… at half time the team receive stress therapy
… there's an uproar of delight if they gain a corner kick
… the club's lucky mascot keeps having freak accidents
… opposition players get sent off for laughing
… there are fewer supporters than players
… they are sponsored by the local Brownies
… the groundsman earns more than any of the players
… all the players are on the free transfer list.

In the middle of the night, the fire-brigade chief calls the Airdrie manager.

"Sir, I'm sorry to have to tell you the stadium is on fire!"

"Oh no!" cried the manager. "Save the cups! Please save the cups!"

"Don't worry," sneered the chief, "the fire hasn't reached the canteen yet."

The Hearts youth coach was asked his secret of evaluating young players.

"Well," he gloated, "I take them into the

woods and ask them to run as fast as they can. The ones that go around the trees, I make into strikers. The ones that run into the trees, I turn into defenders."

Signs that the wean might someday play for Scotland...
✔ The delivery went into extra time
✔ He dribbles constantly
✔ He demands a huge transfer fee when passed from lap to lap
✔ He takes a dive when anyone comes close
✔ He trips up his brothers and sisters
✔ For no apparent reason he keeps spitting

✔ He refuses to pass anything to anyone
✔ He has frequent temper tantrums.

**Phrases a Celtic fan and a Rangers fan
will never utter to each other...**

May the best team win.

*That was never a penalty – our player
took a dive.*

*Although we lost 7-0, I thought the
ref was extremely fair.*

*Congratulations – great win. Your
team was brilliant.*

*Let's swap scarves – I'd be so proud to
wear your team colours.*

Due to a supporters' boycott, a mere 29
people watched Clydebank take on East
Stirling at Greenock Morton's Cappielow
Park in August 1999. Apparently, during
half time, one of the players managed to
get the autographs of every single fan.

Three Aberdeen fans were standing on the
terrace moaning that their team always lost.

"I blame the manager," said the first. "If he'd sign eleven new players we could be a great side."

"I blame the players," said the second. "If they'd make some effort they might at least score a few goals."

"I blame my parents," said the third. "If I'd been born in another town I'd be supporting a decent team!"

Two zealous Elgin fans, sitting cold and miserable in the terrace, were just complaining that the torrential rain and severe fog were making the game even more boring than usual. Indeed there was so little action to be seen that they decided they might as well go for a hot pie and at least heat up a little. Just as they were about to rise from their seats they were interrupted by a police officer. "You lads had best go home now," he declared, "the game was abandoned half an hour ago."

After ten defeats in a row, the frustrated Partick Thistle manager gathered the team together for a serious pep talk. Sarcastically he began, "Those large chunks of wood at the end of the pitch are called goalposts – the object of the game is to get the ball between them."

"Wait, wait," interrupted their latest

signing, "you're going too fast. First of all explain to us – what's a ball?"

On the way home from watching his team being thoroughly thrashed, Douglas spots a fairy drowning in a pond. Bravely Douglas dives in to the rescue, scoops out the little fellow, and places him safely on the grass bank.

"Thanks a bunch," splutters the fairy. "For your good deed I'll grant you a wish."

"Wow!" yells Douglas. "Can I have a huge bundle of gold?"

"Actually," apologises the fairy, "gold's a bit tricky these days – is there maybe something else?"

"Could I have a castle to live in?" enquires Douglas excitedly.

"Are you joking?" replies the fairy. "Have you seen the price of property recently?"

"Okay, okay," says Douglas, "well, you would make me the happiest man in the world if you could just arrange for Kilmarnock to win the league cup."

The fairy hesitates for a few minutes then whispers, "On second thoughts, I might just be able to get you a nice wee castle down the Ayrshire coast..."

Bagpipe Jokes

Bagpipes: The best way to terrorise the neighbours without the risk of getting an ASBO.

Q. What's the difference between a stone of Ayrshire Potatoes and a band of pipers?
A. It only takes twenty minutes to boil the potatoes.

If a piper were playing alone in a forest 100 miles from anywhere – would everyone still hate him?

Q. What's the difference between a piper and a mother-in-law?
A. Not everyone loathes their mother-in-law.

Q. What two things do bagpipes and the Loch Ness Monster have in common?
A. They attract tourists and terrify little children.

Q. What's the difference between a set of bagpipes and Tommy Sheridan?
A. Tommy sues!

Q. How do you get two pipers to play a perfect harmony?
A. Shoot one.

Q. What's the difference between bagpipes and a mother-in-law?
A. A mother-in-law makes a less hideous noise when you blow up her nose.

Q. What do you call a Highlander who hangs around with musicians?
A. A piper.

An officer of the Black Watch, pinned down with his unit in Italy during the

Second World War, urgently signalled his Commanding Officer. "We desperately need reinforcements. Please send a hundred tanks or a couple of pipers."

Q. What's the difference between a bagpipe and an onion?
A. No one cries when you chop up a bagpipe.

Q. What do you throw a drowning piper?
A. His bagpipes!

Q. What is the difference between bagpipes and a squealing pig?
A. The pig has a purpose.

Q. What do you call ten bagpipes at the bottom of Loch Long?
A. A start.

A man wearing a kilt walks into a pub with a suspicious looking parcel under his arms.

"Whit's that?" demands the worried bartender.

"Ten pound o' Semtex," says the kiltie.

"That's a relief," says the bartender, "for a minute Ah thought it was bagpipes."

Q. Why do pipers walk when they play?
A. To avoid being hit by rotten fruit.

Q. What's the difference between a bagpipe and a trampoline?
A. Eventually you get tired of jumping on a trampoline.

Q. If you drop a bagpipe and a lump of shite off Ben Nevis, which smashes up first?
A. Who cares?

Q. What's the definition of "optimism"?
A. A person who plays the bagpipes and yet still owns a mobile phone.

Q. What do you have when a piper is buried up to his neck in sand?
A. Too little sand!

To the delight of the whole of Skye, young Donald wins a scholarship to Oxford University. It's the first time Donald has been away from the island and his parents are naturally worried about him. After a month his father, Donald Snr, makes the long journey down to Oxford to see how Donald is settling into dormitory living.

"Now then my boy, how are you getting on in this foreign country?"

"Oh father," moans Donald, "it's awful. The students on either side of my room are ever so noisy."

"That's not good," says his anxious father.

"On one side there's a girl who screams and shouts all night long and on the other side there's a boy who keeps hitting the wall with a hammer."

"And what do you do about it?" asks Donald Snr.

"I try not to let it upset me," replies Donald, "I just try to keep focused on my bagpipe practice."

Q. Why did the chicken cross the road?
A. To get away from the bagpipe recital.

Q. What is the difference between a piper and a terrorist?
A. Terrorists have sympathisers.

Q. What do you call a piper who can enchant crowds with rapturous music?
A. A pianist.

Q. If you were lost in the woods, who would you trust for directions – an in-tune piper, an out-of-tune piper, or Santa Claus?

A. The out-of-tune piper. The other two are signs that you have been smoking dope.

It's the year 1643 and once again the Scots are about to do battle with the English. This time it's a home game for the Scots and the chosen venue is

Yerrkidden. Three thousand Scots begin marching into battle. At the front of the proud army are the pipers – really giving it laldy. A rain of arrows flies across the open field, ten pipers fall. The pipers bravely march on. Another rain of arrows. This time twenty pipers tumble to the ground but still the pipes ring out. Finally eighty men have fallen. From behind the pipers the chieftain calls out, "For heaven's sake, can you not play something they like?"

Q. What's the definition of a gentleman?
A. One who knows how to play the bagpipes but doesn't.

Q. How can you tell if a bagpipe is out of tune?
A. Someone is blowing into it.

A piper has been hired to do a wedding in Glasgow. On the way he gets lost in the rough East End. He parks his car outside a pub and, leaving his bagpipes on the back seat, nips in to ask directions. When he returns he's shocked to find the rear window broken and another set of pipes dumped on top of his.

Alice and Jane are walking along the banks of Loch Lomond when they hear a high pitched little voice calling, "Help me! Help me!" They look down and see a frog bobbing about on the water on top of a discarded Irn-Bru can.

"I'm a world famous piper. I was turned into a frog by an evil drummer," says the frog. "Kiss me and turn me back to normal – I'll give you all my earnings for the next ten years."

Without hesitation Alice grabs the frog and stuffs him into her pocket.

"You're surely not going to kiss that thing?" asks Jane.

"No way," says Alice. "Ten years of his

salary's worth bugger all but a talking frog will make a mint on eBay."

Q. How do you keep your violin from getting stolen?
A. Put it in a bagpipe case.

Q. What do you call a piper with half a brain?
A. Talented.

Whisky Jokes

Warning Labels that *should* be on whisky bottles

Drinking whisky will make you dance like a retard

Drinking whisky may result in pregnancy

Drinking whisky will make you tell everyone that you love them – over and over and over again

Drinking whisky may leave you wondering what happened to your underwear

Drinking whisky will make even your spouse look sexy

Drinking whisky will make you more attractive to the opposite sex – but only if they're drinking twice as much as you.

The consumption of whisky may create the illusion you are tougher, smarter, faster and better looking than most people.

Don goes into a pub and asks the barman for a shot of whisky. After knocking it back he takes two photos from his wallet, stares at them for a moment and mutters, "Which one of you would I shag?" He orders up another whisky and does the same thing. After doing this six times, he asks the bartender for the bill. The bartender had been watching all of this with great curiosity. As he gives Don his change he asks who's in the photos.

"One of them is my favourite sheep," says Don. "If I want to shag her I know I'm still sober." He takes a photo from his wallet and shows it to the bartender. "But this is my wife – if I want to shag her I know I'm totally pissed."

A man walks into a bar with a slab of asphalt under his arm and says, "A whisky please, and one for the road."

Calan had been out on the town and it was well into the small hours when he was heading home to his little cottage on the outskirts of Fort William. As he goes through a red light he hears the wail of a police siren and moments later is forced to pull over.

"Hellooo," says the officer, "And have we been havin' a bit o' a drink then?"

"Oh aye," says Calan, "well jist a few."

"And how many do we call jist a few?" says the officer.

"Well, Ah had a bottle o' whisky wae ma dinner," says Calan, "An' then at the pub Ah had twelve pints an' another half bottle."

"Och is that all? Sorry for troubling you," says the officer. "Now beware of these traffic lights, they have an awful habit o' changing unexpectedly."

Hamish goes into a posh London bar and asks the bartender if he has a good selection of whiskies. The barman assures him that he has such an extensive cellar he can provide any whisky requested.

"Okay, let's try you out," says Hamish. "Bring me a 1972 Ledaig, please."

The bartender goes down to the cellar and comes back with a crystal glass containing the amber nectar.

Hamish takes a sniff, "Smells beautiful." He takes a sip. "Excellent. May I compliment you on storing the Ledaig in a way that has maintained its wonderful flavour?"

Hamish takes his time savouring the magnificent whisky then asks for a 1964 Clan Denny. The barman disappears into the cellar where, to his horror he discovers that he doesn't have any left. He does, however, have a bottle of 1965 so he returns with a glass of that, thinking that Hamish will never know.

Hamish takes a sniff. "Something's wrong here," he says. He sips the liquid. "My good man – this is a '65 – it's quite different from the '64 due to the wet summer that year."

Embarrassed, the barman offers Hamish the next drink on the house. Hamish thinks for a few moments then requests a 1953 Balvenie Single Barrel.

Worrying about losing his reputation the barman rushes down to the cellar in search of the rare whisky. Much to his relief he eventually finds a bottle. However, he's annoyed at the Scotsman's superior knowledge so he undoes his flies and adds a little extra to the drink. Smirking he returns to the bar and hands Hamish the crystal glass.

Hamish takes a sniff, saying, "An interesting bouquet." Slowly he savours the flavour. "A delight," he proclaims. "It has a vanilla honeyed sweetness with subtle hints of heather and dry oak. I do believe it comes from barrel forty-two."

As the barman stands grinning, Hamish leans over the bar and whispers in his ear, "A wee word of advice, ma' man. Can I suggest you see your doctor tomorrow – I think you might have a dose of gonorrhoea."

Ben is staggering back to his farm after a heavy session at the village pub. It's a foul winter's night, the sleet is sweeping across the fields driving a chill deep into Ben's bones. As he stumbles his way across the rickety old bridge he spots something bright floating in the stream. Thinking it's a Barbie doll he scoops it up with the intention of giving it to his grand-daughter. But to Ben's surprise the little creature wriggles in his hands and says in a high-pitched voice, "Thank you for saving me."

"For Christ's sake!" screeches Ben, "ye nearly scared the shit oot o' me."

"Sorry, sir," says the fairy softly, "I

81

didn't mean to frighten you. For saving my life I shall grant you two wishes."

"Is this thon bloody Candid Camera?" says Ben scanning the trees.

"No, sir," says the fairy, "I am Twinklebum the fairy and I would love to grant you two wishes."

"Aye okay," says Ben, "Ah'll play along wae yer wee game. Gie me a bottle o' everlasting whisky."

There was a POOF and a BANG. A bottle of whisky appears in Ben's hands.

"That wis a neat trick," says Ben, taking a huge drink. "How did you manage that?"

But before the fairy could reply, Ben notices the bottle has filled up again.

"Bloody hell," he hollers, "that's pure brilliant."

"You have one more wish," says the

fairy sweetly. "What else can I get you?"

"What else?" replies Ben. "Ah'll hae another wan o' these please."

Q. What's the difference between a battery and a whisky?
A. A battery has a negative side.

You know you've had too much whisky when...
you try to brush something off your shoulders and find out it's the floor.

The Worst Scottish Jokes

Three Orkney fishermen walk into a bar – you'd think at least one of them would have seen it!

Q. What sits at the bottom of your bed and takes the piss out of you?
A. A kidney dialysis machine.

Then there was the Dundonian who went to buy some camouflage trousers – but he couldn't find any.

Did you hear about the woman from Skye who drowned in a bowl of porridge? *Serves her right for swimming in it.*

Two blokes are in a pub. One turns to the other and says, "Your round." The other replies, "So are you, ya wee fat bastard!"

Jack and John were hunting for deer deep in the forest, miles from anywhere. Suddenly John collapses. He rolls around in agony for ages and then, with a ghastly gasp, becomes lifeless. Jack leans over his friend, who now doesn't seem to be breathing and has turned very pale. Terrified, and not sure how to help his friend, Jack whips out his mobile and dials 999.

"I think my friend is dead!" he yells desperately. "Help me! What can I do?"

"Calm down, don't panic," replies the operator. "Before you do anything you must be sure he's really dead."

The operator holds on as Jack goes to

check his friend. After a long silence the operator hears a shot being fired.

"Is everything okay?" quizzes the operator.

"Aye," replies Jack, "he's definitely dead now."

Scotland's worst air disaster occurred recently when a two-seater Cessna crashed into Glasgow Necropolis Cemetery. Search and rescue workers have recovered 342 bodies so far and expect that number to grow as digging continues.

Q. What's brown and sounds like a bell?
A. Dung!

Sometimes it's so windy on Stornoway that a chicken has to lay the same egg six times.

Old blind Jock and his seeing-dug are in Tesco's doing some shopping. He suddenly stops in the middle of an aisle, grabs the dug by the tail and starts swinging it around above his head. A startled shop assistant rushes over.

"What's up?" she yells, "Can I help you?"

"No, thanks," says Jock still swinging his dug, "I'm just looking around."

Two salmon were in a tank. One said to the other, "Archie, do you know how to drive this thing?"

Sandy was at a cinema watching the old version of *Whisky Galore.* A few rows in front sat a farmer with his Shetland sheepdog. No sooner had the film started than the dog began to laugh hysterically. Within ten minutes the dog was in the aisle, rolling about in fits. Sandy wandered over to the dog's owner.

"That's some dog you have," said Sandy, "I can't believe how much he's enjoying the film."

"Neither can I," said the owner. "He hated the book."

Q. What do you call six weeks of rain in Scotland?
A. Summer!

This big farmer from Fraserburgh goes to see his new doctor. He's shocked to discover that she's a woman, but delighted that she's absolutely drop-dead gorgeous. But when she tells him that he'll have to stop masturbating he's absolutely outraged.

"And why *should* I stop?!" he asks angrily.

"Because I'm trying to examine you," she replies.

Q. What do you get if you cross a thistle and a haggis?
A. A sore throat.

Q. Why do Kwik-Fit only have Protestant fitters?
A. Because all cars now have catalytic-converters.

The Scottish Character

How to impress a Scotswoman
The needs of Scotswomen are very simple – there's no need for expensive gifts of money, diamonds, designer dresses and bouquets of flowers. No, just give up your life, your heart and your soul in devotion to her and she'll be perfectly content. And a few gifts of money, diamonds, designer dresses and bouquets of flowers wouldn't hurt either.

How to impress a Scotsman
The needs of Scotsmen are very basic – there's no need for champagne, cars or designer clothes. No, if you want to create a lasting impression, simply turn up at his house naked with a Haggis

Supper and six cans of Tennent's Lager. Then bugger off and let him get on with watching the footie.

Having a liking for the drink, Jock spent more time at the pub than looking after the haulage company he'd inherited from his father. Soon he was in financial shite. But as he had religiously attended every Celtic home game for the past 40 years, Jock knew that he had a direct line to God. He decided it was time to ask for help. He waited until his wife was fast asleep then knelt down at the side of the bed.

"God, gonnae help me. Ah've nae money left and soon Ah'll lose ma hoose and everything. Be a pal and let me win ra lottery!"

Saturday came – the lottery was drawn – but Jock won bugger all.

He prayed again. "God, they've taken away ma car. Ma company's aboot tae go bust. Gonnae jist dae wan wee thing tae help – let me win yon lottery an' that."

Saturday came – the lottery was drawn and once again Jock won bugger all.

Feeling rather peeved he knelt down for another go at God.

"For Christ's sake God, whit ur ye doin'? Ah've lost ma hoose and business – gonnae gie us a break – let me win ra lottery jist once so Ah can get back oan ma feet!"

Suddenly there is a blinding flash from the heavens.

"Jock ma man," thundered the voice of

God, "see if ye want ma help yer gonnae have tae meet me half way – at least buy a bloody ticket!"

Willie had been nicking out of the Oxfam shop again. The judge asked him if he was guilty or not guilty.

"Och Ah'm guilty," says Willie, "but can we go ahead wae the trial jist tae make sure of it."

Sandy was drinking at a pub all night. When he got up to leave, he fell on his arse. He tried to stand again, but to no avail, falling on his arse again. Slowly he dragged himself outside for some fresh air to see if that would sober him up. Once outside, he tried to stand up and, sure enough, fell flat on his arse. Being a stubborn old codger he crawled all the way home. Once there he crawled up the stairs and into his bedroom. When he reached his bed, he tried once more to stand up. This time he managed to pull himself to his feet but fell onto the bed. He fell asleep as soon as his head hit the pillow.

He woke the next morning to his wife shaking him and shouting, "So, ye've been oot getting blotto again!"

"Nae Ah huvnae," he assured her.

"Ae ye huv!" she yelled. "The pub rang tae say ye left yer bloody wheelchair there again!"

An American tourist is on a walking holiday in the Cairngorms. It's a wild day, there's a mist on the hills and the rain is coming down like cow piss. After struggling with map and compass for several hours he finally admits to himself that he's lost. Luckily a local man spots him and offers to take him to a village where he can dry out and get a bite to eat. As they make their way across hills and along lanes, Jock gives the American a guided tour.

"Dae ye see thon wonderful Scots pines?" asks Phil. "I planted every single one o' them by hand. But dae ye think Ah'm called Phil the Forester? Am I Hell."

A little later, they pass a wonderful building that would put the Palace of Versailles to shame.

"See thon castle over there?" asks Phil. "Took me ten years tae build. But dae ye think Ah'm called Phil the Builder? Am I Hell."

Nearing the village, they see the magnificent clock tower that stands in the village centre. "Dae ye see thon clock?" asks Phil. "Built every bit o' it masel'. Made every cog on ma wee lathe. But dae ye think I'm called Phil the Clockmaker? Am I Hell. But," he continued, "hae sex with just one wee pheasant and yer bloody well branded for life!"

Hard work pays off in the future.
Laziness pays off now.
Old Scottish Proverb

It was the 1st of April – the day of the big blockade at Faslane Naval Base. Peace marchers from all over Scotland had gathered to show their contempt for the English government's policy on nuclear weapons. The protest started in good humour but as the day wore on tempers got hotter. When several people were arrested and carted off, the crowd turned nasty. Throwing bottles and stones they began to force the police back.

"What are we going to do?" asked a young officer.

"Time to call in the Salvation Army," said the Chief.

"Salvation Army? Surely you mean the Army," said the officer.

"No, the Sally Army," replied the chief. "The best way to disperse an unruly Scottish mob is to take up a collection."

Rab had just got himself a job as a Junior Joiner's Mate. It was his first day and he found a cosy corner of the work's canteen to sleep in.

"Whit are ye doin' loafin' around?" yelled the gaffer. "You're supposed tae be cuttin' the timber."

"Och, Ah cannae be bothered," says Rab.

"Whit!" exclaimed the gaffer. "You came tae me yesterday sayin' ye were desperately searching for a job."

"Aye, so Ah did," replied Rab, "but Ah've found one now."

Bono, lead singer of the rock band U2, is famous throughout the entertainment industry for, allegedly, being a right wee pompous git (no offence meant wee man – no need to sue or nothin').

Recently the band was playing a gig in Glasgow. Towards the end of the night, Bono called for total quiet. The lights were turned out – a single spotlight lit up the singer. As the bemused crowd looked on, he started to clap his hands, precisely once every three seconds. After four minutes of this he said slowly into the microphone, "Every time I clap my hands," he gave a loud clap for effect, "a child in Africa dies."

An irate voice from the front of the crowd pierced through the silence…

"Well, stop fuckin' doin' it then, ya murderin' wee cunt!"

"Ah made ma girlfriend cry during sex last night," boasted Sam.

"Oh aye," said David, "and how did you do that?"

"Ah phoned her up while Ah wis shagging her best mate," smirked Sam.

Campbell Campbell was a very proud man. He had two beautiful young daughters whom he loved dearly. But he really wanted a son to carry on the clan name. After months of strenuous effort his wife, Jeanie, fell pregnant and duly delivered a healthy baby boy. But Campbell's joy turned to horror when he laid eyes on the lad – for he was the ugliest baby he'd ever seen. Campbell was furious, convinced the child was not his own. Now all this happened before *Trisha* and DNA testing had been invented, so Campbell called upon the Clan Chief to make judgment.

"Look," said Campbell, "I have the two most beautiful daughters in the whole of Scotland. This ugly child couldn't possibly be mine."

The Clan Chief demanded to speak to Jeanie in private.

"Tell the truth," said the Chief to her solemnly, "or be driven from the village."

"I swear on my mother's grave, I haven't been sleeping around," said Jeanie smiling sweetly. "Well, at least – not this time."

"Oh, Sandy," sighed the wife one morning, "I'm convinced my mind is almost completely gone!"

Her husband looked up from the newspaper and commented, "I'm not surprised! You've been giving me a large piece of it every day for going on twenty years."

One Hallowe'en a wee boy arrives at Bill's door dressed as Rocky in boxing gloves and satin shorts. Bill gave him some goodies, but thirty minutes later the wee boy returned for more.

"Are you no' the same Rocky thit wis here earlier?" asks Bill.

"Aye," says the wee boy, "but now Ah'm the sequel. Ah'll be back three more times the night."

A true story apparently…

A guy walks into a bar in Aberdeen and orders a white wine.

All the hillbillies sitting around the bar look up, expecting to see some pitiful

Tuechter from the north.

The bartender says, "Yer nae fae aroon here loon are ye?"

The guy says, "No, I'm actually from Edinburgh."

The bartender says, "And fit div ye dee in Edinburgh then cheel?"

The guy says, "I'm a taxidermist."

The bartender says, "A taxidermist? Fit the fu*ks a taxidermist? Div ye drive a taxi?"

"No, as a taxidermist I don't drive a taxi. I mount animals."

The bartender grins and shouts to the locals, "It's aricht loons... he's ane of us!"

A Scotsman walking through a field sees a man drinking water from a pool with his hand. "Awa ye eijit, can yeh no tell that's foo o coos keich?!" (Begone you idiot, can't you tell it's full of cow shit?!) The man shouts back, "I'm English. Speak English, I don't understand you!" to which the Scotsman replies heartily, "I said use both hands, you'll get more in!"

At an auction in Glasgow a wealthy American announced that he had lost his wallet containing £10,000 and would give a reward of £100 to the person who found it.

From the back of the hall a Scottish
voice shouted, "I'll give £150!"

A certain private school in Edinburgh
was faced with a unique problem: a
number of 13-year-old girls were
beginning to use lipstick and would put
it on in the bathroom. That was fine, but
after they had put on their lipstick they
would press their lips to the mirror
leaving dozens of little lip prints.

Every night, the cleaner would remove
the lipstick marks and the next day the
girls would put them back. Finally the
Head decided that something had to be
done. She called all the girls to the

bathroom and met them there with the cleaner. She explained that all these lip prints were causing a major problem for the cleaner every evening. To demonstrate how difficult it was to remove the marks, she asked the cleaner to show the girls how much effort was required. He took out a long-handled squeegee, dipped it in the toilet, and cleaned the mirror with it, scrubbing and puffing.

Since then, there have been no lip prints on the mirrors.

There are teachers, and then there are educators.

Cannie Scots Jokes

Kihara made a strong start in the Loch Ness Marathon and even by the mile mark had a decisive lead. However, as he rounded the next corner he was shocked to see a kilted figure a few hundred yards ahead of him. Annoyed that he wasn't in the lead he upped his pace. By the six-mile mark he had reduced the gap enough to see that the leader was carrying a sheep under each arm. Kihara dug in deep but gradually the kilted runner increased his lead again. As he approached the hill at eighteen miles Kihara once again grew close to the leader. Pushing with all his might Kihara drew level at the top of the hill. Through puffs and pants he gasped to the Scotsman, "Why are you making things so difficult for yourself – you could be leading by miles if you weren't carrying those sheep."

"Och Ah'm no' in the race laddie," replied the Scotsman, "Ah jist grudge the bus fare tae take ma sheep tae the market."

Top Tip
Old telephone directories make ideal personal address books. Simply cross out the names and address of people you don't know.

Rory has a wee win on the horses and is taking the trip of a lifetime to Palm Beach in Florida. As he saunters along the beach in his semmit and trackie bottoms, he is amazed by the beauty of the scantily clad women. At last he can take it no more and approaches a stunning blonde.

"Hey doll," he says by way of introduction, "let me suck yer tits an' Ah'll gie ye $200."

"You must be joking," replied the blonde, "it cost me more than that for breakfast at my hotel this morning."

"Awe right then," says Rory, "let's make it $1,000"

"$1,000! This bikini cost me $2000," replies the blond.

"Aye okay then hen – ma final offer is $10,000 – it's awe Ah've goat," pleads Rory.

Feeling sorry for the poor Scots lad

the blonde agrees and they find a secluded stretch of beach. Rory slowly peels off her bikini top to reveal the most perfect breasts in the world.

Gently he caresses them, fondling them slowly and lovingly with each hand. He buries his face in them enjoying their warmth against his cheeks. Then, removing his semmit, he presses his chest against them and enjoys the sweet sensation of her pert nipples pressing into his body.

"Right, that's enough," says the blonde, "Give me my money."

"Money?" says Rory, "But Ah huvnae sucked yer tits yet."

"Well get on with it," demands the blonde.

"Och, Ah don't think Ah'll bother," says Rory.

"What!" roars the furious blonde, "Why not!"

"Because yer too bloody expensive," says Rory as he dauners away.

Phil was thrilled at winning a toilet brush in the office raffle even though it was the booby prize. A few days later a friend asked if he had tried it out.

"I don't like it much," replied Phil. "In fact I'm thinking of going back to using toilet paper."

Peter was delighted at getting a job at Kirkintilloch sewerage but, to the amusement of his co-workers he turned up on his first day wearing his best suit, complete with shirt and tie. It was warm, mucky work so, before long, Peter took off his jacket and hung it over a railing. It slithered off, and began swirling round and round in the vast tank of shite.

As Peter dived in, a co-worker yelled, "It's nae guid doin' that, yer jacket's ruined!"

"Aye, Ah ken fine," replied Peter, "but ma sandwiches are in the pocket!"

Save fuel. Pretend that your car has run out of petrol. There are always plenty of suckers who will help you push it.

Shona MacDonald's husband, Donald, had recently died and she was taking the twelve weans to pay their respects at the grave. But as she approached she spotted Donald's best friend Dugald pissing onto the grave.

"What the hell do you think you're doing?!" she screeched.

"Oh… well I promised Donald that I'd pour a bottle of his favourite whisky over his grave," replied Dugald.

"So why are you pissing on it?" demanded Shona.

"Well," said Dugald sheepishly, "I didn't think he'd mind if I passed it through my kidneys first."

Jamie burst into the house and proudly announced to his dad, "I ran home behind the bus and saved eighty pence."

"You could have done better that that son," replied his father. "You could have run home behind a taxi and saved five pounds."

A fierce Highlander is having a few drinks in an Edinburgh pub. He's about to start on his eleventh beer when he feels the call of nature. Knowing that nothing's safe in an Edinburgh pub, he gets a post-it note and scribbles on it: "This pint belongs to the Inverness Heavyweight Boxing Champion." He then sticks it to the glass.

On his return he sees another note stuck over his. It reads "Your beer is now inside the Edinburgh Marathon Champion. Come and get it."

Sign at a golf course in Aberdeen
Members must refrain from picking up lost
balls until they have completely stopped rolling.

The salesman for a binocular manufacturer was giving a presentation to an Aberdonian Bird Watchers Group. For thirty minutes he expounded on the quality of his products in the hope of securing some good sales.

"Ah think Ah'd better stop you there," interrupted the club secretary, "you're wasting your time – we don't use binoculars at this club."

"But what do you do if you want to get a good look at some birds?" asked the bemused salesman.

"Och, that's simple," said the secretary, "we just stand a little closer to them."

An Englishman, an Irishman and a Scotsman are drinking in a bar in Majorca. The Englishman says, "I wish we were in my local. The beer is real cheap and if you buy one you get one free."

"That's nothing," says the Irishman. "In my local when you buy a Guinness you get two free."

"Big deal," says the Scotsman. "There's

a pub in Perth and when you buy six vodkas they take you through the back for a shag."

"No way!" exclaims the Englishman.

"Aye, I'm not joking," says the Scotsman.

"And have you been to this pub?" asks the Irishman.

"Well no," admits the Scotsman, "but my sister has."

Money Saving Tips

A neighbour's car aerial, carefully bent, makes an ideal coat hanger.

Get two bottles of washing-up liquid for the price of one by putting one in your trolley and stuffing the other in your coat pocket.

If a friend suffers from senile dementia, ten minutes after giving them their birthday present take it from them to use again next year. They'll never know.

Increase the life of your carpets by rolling them up and storing them in the garage.

Save money on loo paper by making use of both sides.

Jimmy, Hugh and Bert are at the pub when a tall, long-haired man comes in and sits at the next table. The three friends are sure they recognise him but can't think where they've seen him before. After another few whiskies, Hugh suddenly nudges his mates and whispers excitedly, "It's Jesus Christ, that's who it is."

"Bloody hell!" replies Jimmy. "You're dead right."

Thrilled at their discovery, they ply the holy guy with Guinness, Tennent's and the very best Buckfast.

Jesus is grateful for all the bewie and every so often looks over and smiles at the three friends. Just before final call, Jesus approaches them. Taking Jimmy by the hand he thanks him for the hospitality.

When he lets go, Jimmy gives a cry of

amazement, "Oh my God! My arthritis is gone! It's a miracle!"

To the delight of the onlookers Jesus takes up some of the sawdust from the pub floor, spits in it and rubs the mix into Hugh's eyes.

"Bloody Norah – I can see better than when I was a ten-year-old."

Jesus smiles at Bert and reaches out to take his arm.

"No way," says Bert, backing off.

"What's wrong, my son?" says Jesus.

"Leave me alone ya big bawbag," bellows Bert, "I'm on disability benefit!"

Top Tip

*If you nick things from designer shops you'll
save much more than nicking out of Oxfam.*

It was a hot summer afternoon in a small
Scottish village and all the men were
pursuing their favourite hobby: drinking
whisky in the pub. Suddenly, the door
bursts open and a man staggers in
panting, his tongue hanging from his
mouth all blistered and swollen.

"What happened, Mac?" asked one of
the regulars.

"Och there wis nearly a disaster," said
Mac. "Ma bottle of whisky fell on the
newly tarred road."

Jock is having lunch in a very posh Aberdonian restaurant where the food resembles art on a plate. As he starts on his tomato soup he notices something odd.

"Waiter," he calls, "there's a fly in my soup."

"I'm dreadfully sorry," says the waiter, "I'll get you another plate."

"Och, it's okay son," says Jock, "I was just checking I wisnae getting charged extra for it."

Agnes was on her death bed. Her husband, Jimmy, was sitting by her side.

"Jimmy… Jimmy," came her faint voice.

"Aye what is it?" says Jimmy.

"Remember on our honeymoon we bought a rare bottle of whisky," says Agnes.

"Aye that was forty-three years ago," says Jimmy. "We put it by for a special occasion."

"This could be our last chance to have it together," wheezed Agnes. "Could you open it?"

"Don't be silly woman," scolded Jimmy, "I'm saving it for the funeral."

Top Tip
Save a fortune on whisky by drinking it from the bottle in the supermarket and putting the empty back on the shelf.

The Rougher Side of Life

An English family was touring Scotland. After visiting Inverness they were heading to Edinburgh but got completely lost. It was getting dark when they reached a busy town so they thought it best to ask for directions. Pulling the car to a halt outside a brightly coloured pub, they rolled down a window and asked a young lad where they were.

"Oh phuck hoff," replies the youth, spitting to the ground.

"Ah Glasgow," says the driver, "And which part of Glasgow are we in, my good fellow?"

"You talkin' tae me ya dobber?" says the youth, testing the car paintwork with his tackety boots.

"Okay – so we're in Dennistoun," says the driver, "and what street would that be?"

"Right ya big shite," says the youth, pulling a knife from his pocket, "you're fur a doin'!"

"Thanks for your help," says the driver, screeching away. "So this is the famous Duke Street..."

The little town of Jedburgh nestles in the rolling hills of the Scottish Borders far enough away from the big cities that it seldom sees any real trouble. The local Neds are content with flashing tourists and throwing stones at cars, so the police close up shop at six o'clock and leave them to get on with it. Then came Shuggie from Govan! Shuggie arrived in town at 2pm and immediately settled himself in a corner of the pub. Quickly most of the tables empty – the locals expecting the big muscle-bound tattooed Glaswegian to turn nasty. By 6pm Shuggie had knocked back a dozen or so Tartan Specials and the barman was checking his insurance.

Shuggie staggers his way into the toilets hurling abuse at anyone who doesn't get out of his way quickly enough. After a pee he returns to his table. He checks his jacket and roars, "Some bastard hus nicked ma wallet!" He knocks over the table yelling, "Ah hud fifty quid in that tae get me back tae Govan. If Ah don't get that money back within the hour, Ah'll need tae dae whit Ah hud tae dae in Moffat and Ah really don't like doing that!"

The barman rushes over and

apologises. He gives Shuggie a few free beers, then convenes an emergency meeting with some wealthy locals.

"Listen," says the barman, "I don't know who took his damned wallet but I don't want no trouble and he looks the trouble type."

"I agree," says Jim the butcher. "Here, I'll chip in a few pounds and let's be rid of the thug."

They all do the same and collect £200, giving it to Shuggie with a sincere apology.

"Well," says Shuggie, "Ah didn't think much o' this toon when ma wallet wis stole, but you guys huv restored my confidence. Ah'll be aff noo."

He heads for the door. Just as he opens it, the barman says, rather timidly, "Can you tell us what you had to do in Moffat that you really didn't like doing?"

Shuggie paused, thinking back on the experience with dread. Slowly he replied, "Ah hud tae walk hame."

Q. Why do pigeons fly upside down over Easterhouse?
A. Because there's nothing worth shitting on.

Q. Teacher: "Darren, what is the longest sentence you can think of?"
A. Darren: "Life, miss."

Q. Did you hear about the Ned who got into Edinburgh University?
A. Someone left a window open.

Callum had just arrived in Glasgow where he would be staying at a little boarding house while attending university. "A word of warning," said the landlord, as Callum headed out to sample the nightlife, "things are a bit rough here in Glasgow. If any hooligans ask you if you're a Tim or a Hun act a bit simple and reply that you're a Partick Thistle supporter."

"Will that stop me getting beaten up?" asked Callum.

"Not completely," replied the landlord, "But they might take pity on you and only break a few limbs."

"Did ye hear thit Jeanie McGeachie's youngest has jist goat his furst ASBO?" said Mary.

"Yur kiddin' – is he no' seven year auld?" asked Alice.

"Aye, that's right," said Mary, "Bit Jeanie always said he wis a slow developer."

Q. Why do Edinburgh residents go to Glasgow car boot sales?
A. To get back their stuff.

Q. What is a Ned's favourite computer game?
A. Electronic tag.

A Ned stops a man on a dark section of Princes Street and bellows, "Gie me awe yer money!"

"How dare you try to rob me!" cries

the man indignantly, "Don't you know I'm an MSP?"

"In that case," snarls the Ned, "gie me awe ma money!"

"That's a beamer o' an eye ye've goat," says Tom, "Whit happened?"

"Och, Ah was daft enough tae invite Gordie round fur Christmas dinner," says Joe.

"Whit? Gordie wae the drink problem?"

"Aye, that's him. He nearly went mental so he did," said Joe. "He thought ma offer o' cold turkey wis dead offensive."

Scottish Lightbulb Jokes

How many Scotsmen does it take to change a light bulb?

21: One to hold the bulb and 20 to drink until the room spins.

2: One to call the electrician and one to pour the whisky.

9: One to change the bulb and eight to find a coin for the meter.

None: Real men ain't afraid of the dark.

5,000,001: One to screw in the bulb and 5,000,000 to mourn that the brave national football team has yet again narrowly missed getting into the next stage of the European / World / Who-Gives-A-Damn Cup.

How many pipers does it take to change a light bulb?

5: One to screw in the bulb and 4 to tell him how much better they could have done it.

101: One to screw in the bulb and 100 to play a mournful, tuneless lament.

2: One to try to play *Scotland the Brave* on the bulb and one to call the psychiatrist.

How many Neds does it take to change a light bulb?

3: One to screw in the bulb and two to nick the ladder.

2: One to replace the bulb and one to hot-wire the electricity supply.

3: One to nick the bulb from Woolie's, one to beat up some random pensioner and one to get blotto on Bucky.

11: One to do it and ten to back him up.

None o' yur fuckin' business ya dobber!

How many Nedettes does it take to change a light bulb?

1: She just holds the bulb up to the socket, and waits for the world to revolve around her.

4: One to change the bulb, one to go for her methadone, one to pick up her Social Security allowance and one to look after her three greetin' Nedlings.

2: One to screw in the bulb and one to act as a character witness at the court case.

2: One to hold the bulb and the other to drink White Cider until the room spins.

**How many Barlanark women does it take
to change a light bulb?**

None. They can't afford lights in
Barlanark.

Scottish Knock Knock Jokes

Knock! Knock!
Who's there?
Ewan.
Ewan who?
You an' me are goin' tae the pub.

Knock! Knock!
Who's there?
Maggot.
Maggot who?
Ma got me a key but Ah lost it.

Knock! Knock!
Who's there?
Thistle.
Thistle who?
Thistle be the funniest ever
knock knock joke.

Knock! Knock!
Who's there?
Shawn the sheep shagger.
Shawn the sheep shagger who.
No – just Shawn the sheep shagger.

Love of Sheep

A Londoner was holidaying near Loch Lomond. One morning he was walking along a country path when he saw a man holding a sheep with its back legs planted in his Wellington boots.

"Are you shearing that sheep?" he asks politely.

"Nay laddie!" says the farmer. "Away an' get yer own."

Q. Why do Aberdonian farmers wear kilts?
A. Because sheep can hear a zipper a mile away.

Q. What's the difference between the Rolling Stones and an Aberdonian farmer?

A. One shouts, "Hey, you, get off of my cloud!" and the other shouts, "Hey, McLeod, get off of my ewe!"

Clive was a journalist with an important London newspaper. Much to his annoyance he was assigned the job of investigating the harsh life on a small island in the north of Scotland. Being a bit of a ladies' man, the first thing he noticed when he arrived on the island was the complete lack of nookie. Over a few pints in the village pub he asked one of the locals, "What do you guys do for romance?"

"If ye mean wimen," said the islander, "we've none on the island. Around here, folks have their carnal pleasure wae sheep."

"That's disgusting!" cried the journalist. "I've never heard of such moral degradation."

However, as the weeks went by, the journalist became randier and the sheep more and more attractive. At last he could take it no longer, so he searched the island for the cutest sheep. He took her back to his flat, bathed and shampooed her then tied pink ribbons in her hair. After a bottle of champagne, he lured Senga the sheep into bed and released his pent-up frustrations – six times. Feeling much better, he decided to take his four-legged lover to the pub for a few whiskies. As he and his woolly friend entered the pub, a hush fell over the patrons and the couple became the object of disapproving stares. Eventually, angered by their reaction Clive jumped to his feet.

"You bunch of bloody hypocrites!" he yelled. "You've been shagging sheep for years, but when I do it, you look at me like I'm some sort of crazy pervert."

"Aye, laddie you're not wrong there," said the barman. "We all shag sheep. But none of us would be brave enough to shag the chieftain's girlfriend."

Glasgow Pub Quiz

Q. What do you call a new riverside development in Glasgow?
A. A slum.

Q. What do you call a Glaswegian with a job?
A. An asylum seeker.

Q. Why wasn't Jesus born in Glasgow?
A. Because God couldn't find three wise men and a virgin.

Q. What do you say to a Glaswegian in a uniform?
A. A Big Mac with French fries, please.

Q. What do you call eighteen Glaswegians crammed into a room ten foot by ten foot?
A. A family.

Q. What do you call a virgin in Glasgow?
A. A tourist.

Q. What do you call a Glaswegian in a suit?
A. The accused.

Q. What do you call a Glaswegian in Edinburgh?
A. Lost.

Q. What's the first question at a Glasgow pub quiz?
A. Who are you looking at mate?

Some Truly Scottish Insults

Ye've goat a face like the back end o' a bus.

Her mind's wandered – it's half way tae Princes Street.

He's one kilt pin short of a full streak.

Ye've goat a face like a weel-kickit ba'.

The wheel's spinning but the haggis is dead.

Ye've goat a face like a wet nicht lookin' for a dry mornin'.

Ye've goat a face like a flittin'.

She's goat less brains than a bag o' bruised fruit.

He's two Gay Gordons short of a ceilidh.

He's a few deep fried Mars Bars short of a square meal.

She's two running rhinos short of a full marathon.

He's goat a tongue like a razor but intelligence like a meat cleaver.

He's two haggis short of a Burns Supper.

He's no the sharpest Skein Dubh in the house.

Why Did the Haggis Cross the Road?

❒ (in Glasgow)... to escape the gangs of razor-flashing Neds.

❒ (in Edinburgh)... to avoid yet another group of moronic Japanese tourists.

❒ (in Inverness)... to avoid being gobbled up by Nessie.

❒ (in Dunfermline)... because there's bugger-all else to do.

❒ (in Selkirk)... to avoid Grace with the knife.

❐ (in Aberdeen)... to avoid being shagged by a randy farmer.

❐ (in Perth)... to catch a bus to... well ANYWHERE!!!

❐ (in Faslane)... to go on yet another futile protest against Trident.

❐ (in Springburn)... to avoid getting eaten by a hoody at the chippy.

❐ (in Larkhall)... to try to find a street without an Orange Lodge.

❐ (in Alloway)... to avoid being the subject of yet another one of Burns' moronic poems.

❐ (in Fort William)... to get out of the constant bloody rain.

❐ (in Bearsden)... to steer clear of the junkies from Drumchapel.

❐ (in Easterhouse) ... to view the posh flats with keypad entry, designed to keep residents in!

❐ (in Campbeltown)... to escape the noise of 1,000 pipers (actually he had to cross sixty roads).

❐ (in Berwick-upon-Tweed)... to escape into Scotland.

❐ (on Iona)... Road? What road?

A MIDGE IN YOUR HAND...
ISBN: 978-1-906051-06-8
£5.99, HARDBACK

THE LITTLE BOOK OF NEDS
ISBN 10: 1-905102-30-5
ISBN 13: 978-1-905102-30-3
£2.99, PAPERBACK

NED SPEAK
ISBN 10: 1-905102-73-9
ISBN 13: 978-1-905102-73-0
£2.99, PAPERBACK

NED JOKES
ISBN 13: 978-1-906051-05-1
£2.99, PAPERBACK

www.crombiejardine.com